THE YEAR OF UNIVERSAL GOOD

Nick Cann

This book is dedicated to

Nick Cann and Robert Pitts

Thank you for making this dream come true.

Once every four years,
On Planet CP-20,
the inhabitants
celebrate a
most wonderful
year.

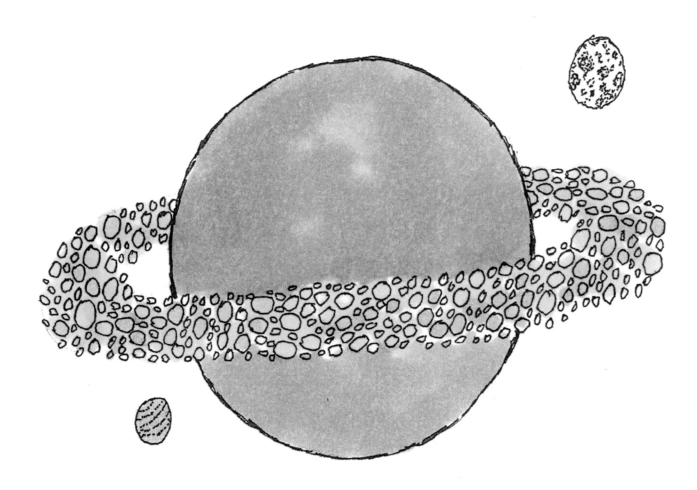

It is called the
Year of Universal Good.

For one full year, the
CP-20's work as hard
as they can to make
their planet as safe,
educated and
healthy as it can
be.

A long time ago, the CP-20's were very selfish and fearful...

They destroyed their economy, society, and future by not looking out for each other.

Pretty soon they all
lived in the planet's
    trash heap.
No one liked the trash heap.

Eventually they got together, and discussed how to make all their lives better.

Some CP-20's were overwhelmed.

But others were super enthused! They helped the overwhelmed CP-20's to overcome their fears and move forward.

Bit by bit they worked together and rebuilt their economy, society and future.

Once the CP-20's got comfortable, they did not become complacent.

Most of the CP-20's realized they would need more than just <u>one</u> year to continue their awesome progress. So they created the year of Universal Good to occur every four years to keep up their momentum.

To keep us moving forward in the future, every four years we will commit one year soley to the purpose of the betterment of our education, safety and health!

The CP-20's also made sure to document the evolution of their society so no one would forget how they got to such a good place, or where they came from.

Every CP-20er has
a planner they keep to
prepare for their
Year of Universal Good.

Project Planner
for
Year of Universal Good

How will you make your world better?

The CP-20's also
give special reverence
to their comrades who
have completed the most
Years of Good.
The more years of GOOD,
the better the pay, the
more accolades.

The CP-20's are happy and proud to say that every CP-20er is healthy, educated and safe. By all working together, the CP-20ers will never return to the Trash Heap of their past.

NOT THE END

Made in the USA
San Bernardino, CA
11 August 2020